P9-EKC-811

Steck-Vaughn

POINT
of
VIEW
Stories

The
Sheriff Speaks

By
Dr. Alvin Granowsky

Illustrated by
Gregg Fitzhugh

STECK-VAUGHN
C O M P A N Y
A Subsidiary of National Education Corporation

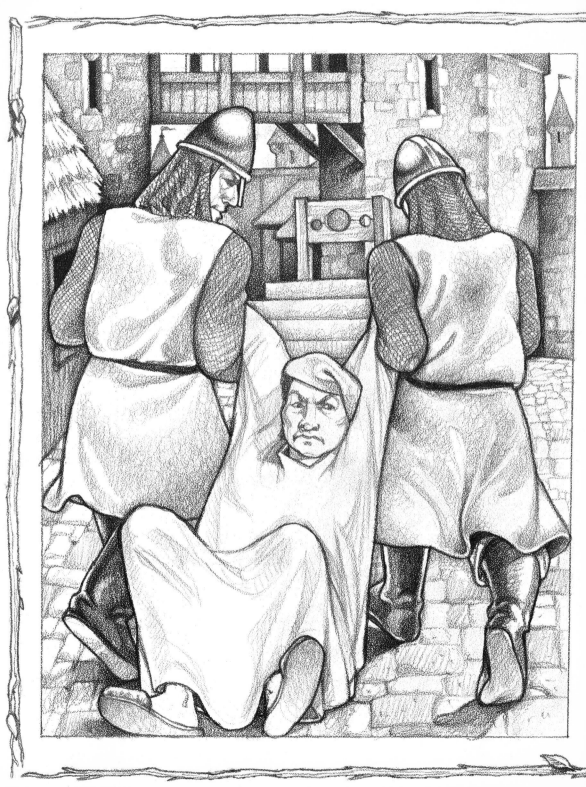

Is it wrong to serve your nation's ruler? If so, I have committed a crime. But nay, I say! I was an honorable man doing an honorable job. I was the Sheriff of Nottingham. I had justice to uphold. And uphold it I did. I made every effort to rid the country of its worst criminal and traitor—Robin Hood. For my efforts I was yanked from my bed, dragged through the town in my nightclothes, and thrown into the stocks. Now I ask you—is that proper treatment for a man who has served his country faithfully? Nay, I say. Nay!

The poor people of this country fawn over Robin Hood and claim he is a hero. He is no hero, I say. He is a common thief. Some say he is an honorable thief because he tosses a few coins to the poor now and then. But again, I say nay! There is no such thing as an honorable thief. Thievery is thievery all the same.

You've heard the story that rotten Hood tells. People who are taken in by his story pay no heed to mine. But I have faith that one day people of reason will hear me out. My tale will prove that honor is on my side.

At birth Robin Hood was named Robert Locksley. He changed his name after the first time he broke the law. Some say he was noble to steal from the rich and give to the poor. Nay, I say. What noble man takes what is not his and hides behind an assumed name? Only a coward would do that!

As the Sheriff of Nottingham, I was loyal to the leader of my country. At that time England's ruler was Prince John. King Richard had abandoned the country and left his brother John to reign. The prince counted on me to uphold order in the land. I vowed that England would become a country where honest people need not live in fear of outlaws. If anyone was afraid, I wanted it to be the outlaws.

To restore law and establish order, I had to find out who was a threat to the prince. At this time Locksley had not yet taken to calling himself Robin Hood. But he had been heard speaking against Prince John and proclaiming King Richard the rightful leader. I had Sir Guy of Gisborne follow the traitor.

In no time Gisborne caught Locksley in a traitorous act. Locksley shot a doe that belonged to the prince. What a cowardly deed to leave a fawn without its doe! If that scoundrel denies it, he is not only a coward but also a liar. Pay him no heed. Witnesses will swear to his dastardly deed. Gisborne and his men surrounded Locksley. But before they could take him back to Nottingham to receive the punishment he deserved, the robbers of Sherwood Forest arrived.

The thieves closed in on Gisborne and his men. Will Scarlet, a true brigand and the leader of the outlaws, ordered his men to grab Locksley and drag him into the forest.

The scoundrels bound Gisborne and his men to their horses and sent them riding to town. The outlaws rode off to their campsite and took Locksley with them. No one was sure of Locksley's fate. Gisborne thought that Will Scarlet might have killed Locksley. If he had, I would have considered it a favor.

But instead of being killed, Locksley joined up with those criminals. And criminals they were. They started a reign of terror upon the good people of England. Locksley replaced Will Scarlet as the leader of the band. He began calling himself Robin Hood. Soon citizens of noble birth fell victim to those shameless thieves. No purse was safe. The good people of Nottingham suffered greatly at the hands of Robin and his hoodlums. "Merry men" they were called. They ran merrily about the country committing crimes. Innocent people found acorns in their money sacks instead of coins. Respected merchants had their purses cut from their belts. Hood and his band stole bags of gold from the royal carriages. No traveler could feel safe when journeying near Sherwood Forest.

The crimes that Hood and his crew committed were an outrage. Of course, I did everything a good sheriff could do to stop them. Many times I almost caught them. But those outlaws were a crafty lot, and they always found some devious way to escape.

The band of outlaws grew. It swelled to the size of an army. Misfits of every description found a home with Hood. Even a man of the cloth, Friar Tuck, involved himself with the scoundrels. At first we thought the friar might be trying to return the thieves to lawful ways. But then I learned that he led the raids on St. Mary's Abbey. He should be condemned for his deeds. A man of his position turning to crime is an outrage!

Not satisfied with his band of outcasts, Hood began recruiting other malcontents. Lady Marian Fitzwalter was only too glad to join up. Such a foolish girl! Her family should have controlled her. They should have forced her to marry Gisborne as she was supposed to. But instead of forcing her to do anything, they let her run wild through the forest with that bunch of hoodlums. I heard that when she tried to join the band, Hood did not even recognize her. What an idiot he is! What kind of fool cannot recognize someone he has known since childhood? When he didn't see through Lady Marian's simple disguise, she flew into a rage. She drew her sword. I hear Marian sliced the simpleton. What a pity she didn't finish him off then and there!

Soon enough, Lady Marian's anger gave way to poor judgment, and she married the dolt. They had some foolish forest ceremony performed by that ridiculous Friar Tuck. Gisborne went mad when he learned what she had done. I have no time for matters of the heart. But Gisborne's broken heart made him hate Hood more. Gisborne dedicated even more time and attention to capturing that scoundrel Hood.

It was not enough that Hood had led astray the foolish Lady Marian. He recruited people of all ages for his dastardly band. He enlisted a grandmother and her three grandsons to take part in his crimes. He trained them to make a living by stealing.

I remember well the day the three little thieves were dragged before me. "What is the problem?" I asked the merchant who had nabbed them.

"These thieves have stolen from my shop!" he said.

"What have they stolen?" I asked.

"An egg!" said the merchant.

"If it's an egg today, it will be a chicken tomorrow!" I spoke from experience with that sort of boy. "We must make an example of them for all young thieves of England. Hang them in the public square!"

As I left the boys in my soldiers' care, their miserable grandmother threw herself on the ground before me. She begged forgiveness for her boys. She made a scene to gain the sympathy of the townspeople. "They are little boys!" she cried. "Please pardon them! Give them one more chance!"

No fool myself, I knew exactly what the old woman was doing. I would not be taken in by it.

"One more chance?" I spoke loudly so all the rabble could hear. "Another chance to become more skilled at the thievery you teach? Another chance to victimize the good citizens of Nottingham? They stole an egg! The hanging is decreed and will take place as planned."

The listening crowd grew restless. They gathered about me as if to do harm. But I, the Sheriff of Nottingham, was no coward. My duty was to enforce the laws of Prince John and England. I had no time to worry about what people thought of me. "Drive off that rabble," I called to my soldiers. "Kill any who resist!" Then I went about my affairs.

On the day of the hanging, I went to the square where the gallows had been raised. The rabble had also returned. I was immediately suspicious. The commotion I heard was more than just the expected noise of the beggars and thieves gathered to watch a hanging.

The crowd grew quiet when the little thieves were brought out. I sensed something was about to happen. But before I could act, the outlaws began their attack. Arrows rained down upon us. I tried to maintain order, but the crowd was wild. In the confusion the boys were cut free. The little thieves disappeared into the crowd and joined Hood's band.

After that incident, the prince demanded the capture of Hood and his men. **And** his woman—"Maid Marian," as she was called. She turned out to be as criminal as the rest of them. She was the one who cut the young thieves free that day. Gisborne should have been glad to be rid of that girl.

I had to find a way to seize the band and jail them. So you can imagine my delight when one of the outlaws appeared at my door.

I had just sat down to a bowl of soup when a loud knock at my door rudely interrupted my supper.

"Who is it?" I asked.

"It is Little John from Sherwood Forest," he said.

I recognized the man, though I knew him by his real name—John Little. When he was a child, he was caught stealing firewood. When his thievery was brought to my attention, I was too soft on him. Back then I believed a bit of punishment could change a boy. I gave the rascal twenty lashes with a whip. Just twenty, not one lash more. The punishment fit the crime. The whip drew blood but did not touch the boy's conscience. As I whipped him, he stood tall and smug as if he were a prince rather than a common thief. He should have been hung for his crime. But I spared his life. Did John Little or his family show any gratitude for my effort to reform the boy? Nay, they never did. When I saw him standing at my front door, I thought that he had finally come to thank me for sparing his life.

"Yes, John Little," I said. I called him by his proper name. "What brings you to the house of the Sheriff of Nottingham, my boy?"

He was really no longer a boy. He had grown into a giant. A giant thief, I knew. But I purposely called him a boy to remind him of the years that I'd known him.

"Sheriff," he began, "a magnificent stag lives in Sherwood Forest. The likes of it have not been seen before. I came upon it by chance when I was gathering firewood. I thought it only fitting that our honored sheriff be the one to take it down. It will make a fine feast for your table."

I agreed that I should be the one to hunt the stag. I thought this was John Little's way of repaying his debt to me for my leniency of years past. When he mentioned gathering firewood, I knew I was right. I was glad to hear that he was now getting his firewood by honest means instead of stealing it the way he did as a child.

"Tomorrow should be a fine day for the hunt, Sheriff," he said. "Will you come?"

"I'll be there," I said.

The next morning I met John Little at the edge of the woods as I had promised. We soon spied a mighty rack of antlers. I drew closer. Just as I realized that the antlers were not on a stag but on Hood, I found myself surrounded by hoodlums. They trapped me!

Because of John Little's deception, I became the captive of Hood and his band of thieves. A lesser man might have begged for mercy. But not I! I endured their torment without a sound. They dragged me to their camp. They mocked me all the way, but I paid them no mind. I answered with silence. They thought they could annoy me, the Sheriff of Nottingham, with a few jibes. But nay, I say. Nay!

Hood and his crew went to great lengths to mock me. They served me dinner on fine silver stolen from my cupboard. I don't know why they stole my silver—they have no appreciation for fine things. They are so uncivilized they ate with their hands! While they gave me only stale bread and water, they gorged on a huge meal that smelled delicious. They were rude gluttons, the lot of them!

After dinner they left me to sleep on the ground with a huge oak root poking into my flank. But I would have none of it. Before those thieves could cut my throat, I escaped their clutches. When I was sure they were asleep, I burst out of the ropes that bound me. One of the hoodlums woke up when he heard me stir. He stumbled toward me. I thrashed him quickly. He fell and several of the others awakened. They charged me, but I battled them all and won. As Hood tells it, they sent me back to town. But nay, I say! They are ashamed that I was able to overpower the whole lot of them and escape. But escape I did, and back to town I went. As soon as I reached town, I met Gisborne to devise a plan. I was determined to see the downfall of Robin Hood, John Little, and the rest of the raiders.

Gisborne and I organized a public contest of skill at shooting the bow and arrow. We knew such a contest would appeal to Hood's conceit about his ability as an archer. His pride would require him to compete. Once he did, we would capture him AND his band of thieves.

Gisborne and I let it be known throughout the land that the prize for this contest was a golden arrow. Gold is what Hood coveted most of all—though he had stolen enough of it to fill a royal palace.

When the day of the contest arrived, the thieves appeared as we knew they would. Robin Hood and Maid Marian wore ridiculous disguises. They imagined us to be fools, but we immediately saw through their act. When I spotted John Little hiding in the crowd, I signaled to Gisborne.

As fine an archer as Robin Hood is, he was no match for Gisborne. Hood's arrow hit the bull's-eye. But Gisborne's arrow split Hood's arrow in two. Their leader being bested caused quite an uproar among the robbers of Sherwood. Later they even took to telling the story backwards. They say it was Hood's arrow that split Gisborne's arrow in two. That is fiction. I saw the contest myself, along with a crowd of others.

As soon as Gisborne made the winning shot, John Little yelled out in anger. I knew trouble might start so I nodded to Gisborne. He shot an arrow, hitting John Little in the leg. Hood and Maid Marian disappeared, leaving the wounded John Little at our mercy. What kind of leader abandons one of his own? A wounded man at that! His actions are only more proof that Hood is a coward. Even though he left John Little behind, I knew Hood valued the brute. Gisborne and I set out to use John Little as bait to capture Hood once and for all.

As Gisborne and I rode to Sherwood Forest dragging John Little behind us, we saw the man's true character. The giant oaf whined the whole way into the woods. Unpleasant as it was, I endured his sniveling in order to catch Hood.

I was prepared to have my men attack Hood and his horde. But Gisborne wanted to talk with Hood alone. "I shall go to speak to Hood. Perhaps reason will win out and bloodshed can be avoided," he said. "If that cannot be, I shall slay Hood and sound my horn."

I decided to let Gisborne try to reason with Hood. As events proved, though, you cannot trust a criminal such as Hood. As Hood came out from hiding, Gisborne dismounted and reached out his hand in greeting. He tried to speak reasonably to the outlaw.

But instead of responding with reason, Hood acted as a coward. With one thrust of his sword, Hood killed Gisborne in cold blood.

As further proof of his deceit, Hood sounded Gisborne's horn. That signal should have meant Hood was finally dead. But it was Gisborne who lay in the forest, not Hood. Hood dressed in Gisborne's cloak and rode out to find me. I studied the rider galloping toward me, and saw through the charade. I realized it was my duty to kill Hood. I planned to slay him the instant he rode up to me. But unfortunately, his ruffians ambushed me and took me hostage.

I had no idea what my fate would be, but I was not afraid. While four brutes held me, so that I had no way to protect myself, John Little kicked me with all his might.

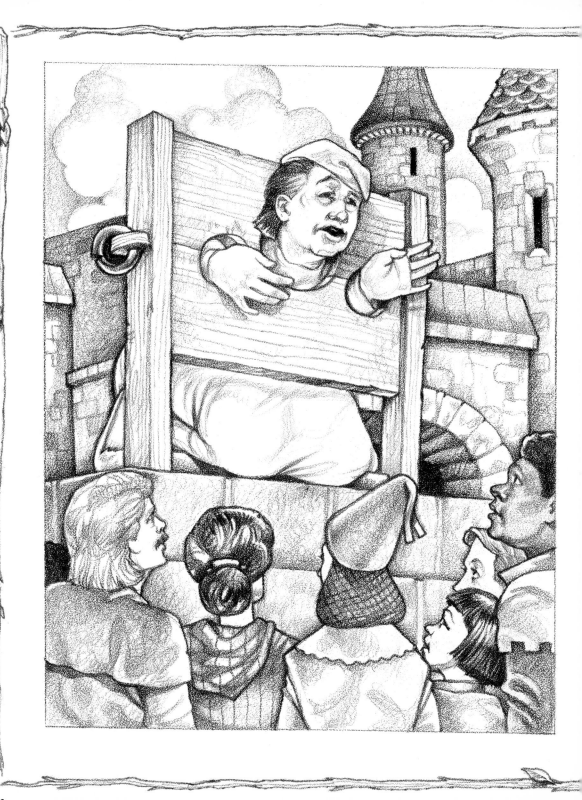

I did not flinch at his assault. I turned to John Little and said, "So this is my reward for sparing your life when you were a child. Without Hood and his army to protect you, you would never dare to treat me thus. You are nothing but a coward." Although I refused to let him see it, John Little's attack on me was infuriating. My anger gave me the strength to break away from the riffraff that held me. I left hoodlums laying on the ground and returned to Nottingham with my head held high. Though they outnumbered me, I had once again overcome them.

The rest is history. As soon as the irresponsible King Richard returned to England, he took power. He invited that thief Robin Hood and his wayward wife to train his army in shooting the longbow. I can't imagine such a thing! A criminal training the royal army. That is absurd! And should the prince of thieves replace the true prince? Nay, I say. But Prince John and his followers were overthrown. That included me, of course. I was thrown out of office and into these stocks. I do not belong here, I say! It is Robin Hood and his band of thieves that deserve such treatment, not me. Is this a fitting treatment for an honorable man doing an honorable job? Nay, I say. Nay!

Steck-Vaughn
POINT
of
VIEW
Stories

Robin Hood

A Classic Tale

Retold by
Dr. Alvin Granowsky

Illustrated by
David Griffin

STECK-VAUGHN
C O M P A N Y
A Subsidiary of National Education Corporation

In England of old, near a great forest, nestled a town called Nottingham. Those who lived there prospered. All was well until the good King Richard left the land to fight the Holy Wars. In his absence, Prince John challenged his brother's reign. While greedy nobles prospered under the prince's command, the lot of the common people grew desperate. The prince was a tyrant who depended on henchmen to enforce his injustices.

To carry out his harsh decrees, the prince relied on two men in particular—the Sheriff of Nottingham and Sir Guy of Gisborne. Both men saw a chance to improve their own lot by forming an alliance with Prince John. They desired the land and fortune bestowed on those loyal to the prince. They would stop at nothing to further John's cause.

Young Robert Locksley fell victim to these men. As the handsome youth walked through Sherwood Forest one day, he chanced upon a doe and her fawn. Taken by their beauty, Locksley paused to watch the animals. Suddenly, an arrow soared through the trees, piercing the doe's heart. Locksley was shocked at this cruelty. He cried out in anger, "Who thinks it just to leave a fawn without its doe?"

In the next moment, Locksley had his answer. He found himself facing armed men pointing arrows at him. "You dare to poach our master's deer!" the leader accused.

Locksley was shocked at the lie. "Never!" he said.

"Tell that tale to the Sheriff of Nottingham," the leader said. "He may believe you. But 'tis more likely that he will believe his own—those who saw you slay that deer."

Locksley knew the leader to be the ruthless Sir Guy of Gisborne. No gain could be gathered from trying to reason with this knave. Sir Guy had long coveted Locksley Farm. With Locksley jailed, Sir Guy could seize the land.

Sir Guy's lackeys bound Locksley's hands with a rope. Sir Guy himself tied the rope to his saddle and kicked his horse into a trot. "Let those who look know the fate of poachers!" he said. Locksley was dragged through the dirt.

Suddenly, thieves dropped from the trees. "The robbers of the greenwood!" Robert thought.

"Dare to move and 'tis death for all!" a tall thief said. "Should none of you follow, only the doe-killer will die!" At his signal, Locksley was dragged into the woods.

As Locksley was stolen away, a robber ordered Sir Guy and one of his men to get on a horse. Then the robber bound the two men back to back. With a slap to the horse, Sir Guy was returned to town in disgrace.

Once back at the outlaws' camp, the bandits released Locksley. As the men gathered around a fire, Locksley began his story. "Locksley Farm was my inheritance. Sir Guy has long wanted it. He tried to steal it from my father. His cohort, the sheriff, raised the taxes to an amount that almost emptied our coffers, but we kept the land. Now they plan to lock me away for a crime I did not commit and then take Locksley Farm. They will make me out to be an outlaw while they steal what is rightfully mine."

"'Tis no shame to be an outlaw in these times. So much wickedness has been imparted in the name of the law!" said Will Scarlet, who had led the ambush in the woods.

"Down with Prince John! Down with the sheriff!" roared the men sitting around the fire.

"The backs of the poor are being broken by these tyrants," Robert said softly. "And what is more, those who protest the greed and cruelty are killed or thrown into jail."

"What think you, Robert Locksley? Will you join our efforts to return justice to our land?" Will Scarlet asked.

"Yes," Robert answered. "I could think of no vocation finer than to serve justice well. We must take from the rich and return what has been stolen from the poor. That is just, and I would be proud to add to your efforts."

Will Scarlet spoke again. "Forgive the rough treatment you received at our hands. 'Tis best if the sheriff believes you dead. Thus, you would be wise now to live as someone else." He smiled. "Will Scarlet is not my given name. All the Men of Sherwood change their names to protect their families. You will need a new name fitting for a life in the forest. What shall it be? Robin O'Wood?"

Locksley thought for a moment. "A fitting name for a man in hiding . . . " Then he pulled his cloak over his head and looked at the men around him. "I shall be Robin Hood," he said with a smile.

Henceforth, he was Robin Hood. In the passing seasons, he learned the way of the woods and the culture of the outlaws living there. Robin was quick-witted, fair-minded, courageous, and skilled with the bow and arrow. Most important of all, Robin was a natural leader.

Soon the small group of robbers swelled to a multitude. Men of every description joined forces with Robin. A huge man called Little John, a friar named Tuck, and the loyal Will Scarlet were Robin's most trusted allies.

In a surprisingly short time, Robin Hood turned a ragged lot into a highly trained army. They were committed to one cause: righting wrongs. They took from the rich to give to the poor. Many a starving family lived because of the sack of food or purse of coins found on their doorstep.

The common folk of Nottingham loved Robin Hood because of his deeds. But their hearts were filled with hatred for the corrupt Sheriff of Nottingham. Among themselves, the commoners ridiculed him as the prince's puppet. The sheriff seemed powerless against Robin and his men. He did not enjoy being taken for a fool, and he vowed to punish all who mocked him. Robin vowed to protect any the sheriff attacked.

One night an old woman came to Robin's camp. "Robin Hood!" she cried. "I need your help!"

"Good woman," replied Robin. "What do you seek?"

"My grandsons have been imprisoned by that murderous Sheriff of Nottingham," she sobbed.

"What was their crime?" Robin asked quietly.

"They were hungry, and they took an egg," said the old woman. "The sheriff says they will die for this crime. They are just children. They don't deserve to die! They have no mother or father, and I am barely able to feed them."

"I understand," said Robin. "It seems that justice left the land with King Richard. But justice will prevail for your boys. They will not die at the sheriff's hands. Of that be assured."

The next day Nottingham bustled with activity. The gallows had been raised in the center of the town. A crowd gathered to watch. The area in front was reserved for the sheriff and his guests. The sheriff took his seat. Sir Guy of Gisborne and Lady Marian Fitzwalter joined the sheriff. Lady Marian looked less than happy to be with Sir Guy. But no one was more unhappy than the three little boys sentenced to hang. They were brought out with blindfolds covering their eyes. The crowd watched the boys in sadness.

Suddenly, a peddler reached into her basket and brought out a horn. As she sounded it, a shower of arrows descended on the platform. In the mayhem that followed, the peddler jumped onto the platform. Her skirt caught on a board and ripped. As the peddler's disguise fell away, the people understood exactly who had begun the assault.

"Robin Hood!" went up a cheer from the crowd.

As all eyes turned to Robin, Lady Marian slipped from her seat and wended her way toward the boys. She pulled a small dagger from her sleeve and sliced the ropes that held the boys prisoner. With a push from Marian, the boys fell from the platform into the arms of Little John. With Robin in the lead, his tribe bravely fought their way out of the village. Infuriated by the escape, the sheriff thought of nothing but capturing Robin Hood from that day forth.

Seeing the young boys at the gallows reminded Little John of his first encounter with the sheriff. When Little John was just nine years old, the pompous sheriff punished him for taking a log of firewood. The sheriff whipped the boy without mercy. Little John still bore the scars. As John grew into a man, he saw many of the poor mistreated by the sheriff. Little John was determined to repay the sheriff for the suffering he had caused.

One day Little John went to Robin with a plan to teach the sheriff a lesson. Robin agreed to the plan. The plan was set into motion.

Little John lured the sheriff into Sherwood Forest under the guise of hunting a giant stag. In no time, the haughty sheriff spied a magnificent pair of antlers. As he drew closer, though, the sheriff realized that the antlers graced Robin Hood rather than a mighty stag. Robin's fellows surrounded the sheriff and tied his hands. They led the sheriff through the forest to their camp. They took many turns and twists to confuse their captive about their camp's location. The sheriff arrived flushed and exhausted. "Sit down to feast at our table set with silver," said Robin.

As the wide-eyed sheriff watched, Little John carried out an elegant silver tray. "Do you like our silver?" he asked.

"Where would the likes of you get silver?" snapped the sheriff. "No doubt 'tis stolen from some unfortunate traveler."

"You are right. It would seem more fitting in a home such as yours," said Little John. He laughed at the expression on the sheriff's face. It was clear that the sheriff recognized the silver as his own—taken from his table!

That night, the men forced the Sheriff of Nottingham to sleep in the brush. "You'll find no feather beds in the forest," said Robin. "Tonight you shall sleep on the ground."

The next morning Robin said, "We hope you enjoyed our hospitality, Sheriff. But now we fear it must end. Before I bid you farewell, you must pay what is due. When we have wealthy guests, they always leave a rich stipend in return for our hospitality."

Robin turned to his men. "Relieve the good sheriff of his gold. Then return him safely to his home."

The men freed the sheriff near his house. He was furious. "Robin Hood and his troop of thieves will hang for this!" he vowed. "They will swing from the gallows in the square!"

In the days that followed, Robin and his men took care not to be recognized. They knew they had angered the sheriff. They moved quietly and cautiously for the sheriff's spies were all about. So when Robin Hood came upon a fine-featured youth at the edge of the forest, Robin hid his face with his cloak. "Danger lurks in this forest. 'Tis not safe for children," he said to the lad.

"I am no child!" said the youth. "I am here to join Robin Hood."

"That villain!" said Robin.

"He is no villain!" said the youth as he drew his sword.

"I refuse to fight children!" Robin said. He turned to walk away.

Without another word, the youth lunged at Robin. Robin leapt back to avoid the blade. He drew his sword to defend himself. The youth struck angrily. The two fought fiercely, each showing skill with the sword. Robin had to use all his ability to hold his own. Then the youth's blade slid past Robin's guard and sliced Robin's face, drawing blood. Robin's sword scraped the youth's hand.

As Robin wiped the blood from his face, his hood fell back.

"Robin Hood!" the youth exclaimed.

"The villain himself!" Robin said. "And who are you?"

"Have you never seen me before?" asked the youth, removing his cap. Thick, black curls tumbled about a comely, girlish face. It was his childhood friend.

"Lady Marian Fitzwalter!" Robin was aghast. What if he had harmed her! He was surprised to see the brave girl. "Have I hurt you?" he asked.

"'Tis but a scratch," said Lady Marian. "I am here to serve your cause, Robin Hood, for you stand for what is right." She paused before continuing. "As you may know, my father pledged my hand in marriage to Sir Guy of Gisborne. But I will not obey my father's wishes! Sir Guy and that sheriff are the cause of what is cruel and evil in this land! I will not marry such a man. I beg you, Robin, allow me to stay here with you."

"It would gladden my heart if you did," Robin said.

So Robin welcomed Marian to the clan, but his men did not think it seemly for a lady to join their army. At first, they stood firm in their opposition to her. But as Marian bested one after another with the sword, she won each man's grudging admiration. They named her Maid Marian. In time, few remembered that their fearless, young colleague had once been the genteel Lady Marian Fitzwalter.

After a time, Robin Hood and Maid Marian were married in the greenwood. They knelt side by side in the heart of the forest and exchanged vows. Friar Tuck, the monk who lived with Robin's brood, performed the ceremony. Robin and Marian's union delighted all in the forest. Clearly, the two were meant for one another. Each had been born of noble birth. Each had given up a privileged life to fight injustice.

When the sheriff learned of the marriage, he turned to Sir Guy. "Was she not promised to you, Gisborne? The thief has stolen her heart from you, I'd say," the sheriff sneered.

From that day forward, Gisborne's hatred for Robin raged through him like a fire through the forest. Sir Guy was bent on revenge. He doubled his efforts to capture Robin and his gang of outlaws.

The sheriff and Sir Guy laid a trap to catch Robin Hood. They announced a contest of skill with the bow and arrow. They would award an arrow of solid gold to the best marksman. Both felt that Robin and his outlaws would surely attend the event to show off their skills.

On the appointed day, the best archers stood ready to compete. Robin Hood was not among them. The sheriff and Sir Guy feared their plan had failed.

A stooped, old man limped up to the archers. A curly-haired lad ran to the old man's side. "Grandfather, you should be at home," he said.

"Cannot an old cobbler aim as well as a knight?" he asked in a feeble voice.

"You may compete, old man," sneered Sir Guy. "Let the contest begin!"

Several archers hit the target. Sir Guy, excellent with the bow, had the best showing. His arrow hit the bull's-eye. Then the old cobbler took steady aim. The arrow flew into the bull's-eye, splitting Sir Guy's arrow in two.

"One lucky shot does not make a winner!" responded Sir Guy. "The winner is determined by three!"

So began the second shot. The old cobbler again bested the field. "Well shot!" yelled a voice from the crowd. The sheriff recognized the voice of Little John. The sheriff whispered his discovery to Sir Guy. Indeed, the ruffians of Sherwood Forest had come to the match.

On the third shot, the cobbler again hit the bull's-eye. The crowd roared its approval. Then Sir Guy took aim. At the last instant, he whirled and shot the arrow toward Little John, who fell with an arrow deep in his thigh.

"Seize the cobbler!" the sheriff shrieked. But while all eyes were upon the fallen Little John, the cobbler reached for his grandson. "We must make all speed, Marian," Robin said as they fled. The golden arrow lay unnoticed—unclaimed by its rightful winner.

Robin Hood escaped, but the wounded Little John became the sheriff's captive. "Make for Sherwood Forest," ordered Sir Guy. "Robin Hood dare not attack while we hold Little John."

The sheriff's pudgy face tightened with fear. He had not forgotten the fearful night he spent among the outlaws.

"Bring the prisoner with us," replied the sheriff. Little John would be their shield and their bait.

As they entered the forest, Sir Guy rode ahead of the others. He lowered his helmet over his face so that only his piercing eyes showed. When he reached the heart of the forest, he called out, "Sir Guy of Gisborne has come to meet Robin Hood in honest combat."

Robin Hood stepped out from behind a tree. "I am the man you seek," he said.

Sir Guy looked at Robin as if he were seeing a ghost. "Robert Locksley! So you are the coward who hides behind the name Robin Hood. I might have known you were not dead. But that will change quickly!"

Sir Guy leapt from his horse, and the two men battled with swords. The sinister Sir Guy was a fierce swordsman. Many a foe had fallen by his blade. It took all of Robin's skill to ward off Sir Guy's murderous lunges. Suddenly, Robin's sword reached its mark—the sword pierced Sir Guy's evil heart.

Robin knelt before the lifeless Sir Guy. "You left me no choice, Gisborne. 'Twas kill or be killed. I am not yet willing to die." Robin donned Sir Guy's cape and helmet. Then he sounded Sir Guy's hunting horn.

The sheriff heard the horn. "The kill is made. Robin Hood is dead!" he said. He waited for Sir Guy to join him.

Robin mounted Sir Guy's horse and rode to meet the sheriff. As the rider approached, the sheriff cried, "The villain is dead!"

"You are right. The villain is dead!" said Robin. He removed his helmet.

The sheriff collapsed in fear. "I beg you, Robin Hood! Do me no harm! I have gold . . . "

"Release Little John!" demanded Robin. "If he dies, you shall welcome death before I am through with you!"

"Release the prisoner!" the sheriff shrieked.

But Little John needed no release. At that very moment, he walked into the clearing, dragging two of the sheriff's men behind him.

"What think you, Little John—life or death for the sheriff?" Robin asked.

"I would not dirty my sword with his blood," said Little John. "Be gone, coward!"

Defeated, the sheriff and his men carried Sir Guy's body to Gisborne Castle for burial. Sir Guy no longer lived, but other wicked ones replaced him. England continued to suffer under the harsh rule of Prince John. Some believed the good King Richard was in prison or had died in the Holy Wars. The country longed for his return. Robin and his merry band fought injustice at every turn.

One day as Robin walked through the woods alone, he met a tall stranger wearing the hat of a pilgrim.

"I seek Robin Hood," said the stranger. "I want to see the man who does not uphold the king's laws."

"He upholds the laws of the true king, but not those of the impostor," replied Robin.

"Does he anger the Sheriff of Nottingham?" asked the stranger.

"Yes," said Robin, "by saving innocent children from the gallows."

"I want to meet this man," said the stranger.

"You have," replied Robin. "I am Robin Hood."

Robin and the tall stranger returned to the camp. When the pilgrim removed his hat, Robin Hood stared intently at the face that seemed familiar. There was no mistaking that face, though its lines told of great suffering.

"King Richard!" exclaimed Robin. "At last you return!" Robin knelt before him.

"Long live King Richard!" the Men of Sherwood shouted. Following Robin's lead, they knelt before their noble king.

"I have returned to punish those who steal and murder," said the king.

"We steal from the rich to return to the poor. We kill only to save ourselves," Robin explained.

King Richard laid his hand upon Robin's shoulder.
"Stand up, Robert Locksley, also known as Robin Hood
of Sherwood Forest. I pardon you and your men. You
have been brave and just. Now I will give you a special
commission. You and your finest archers must come with
me to London. My soldiers lack the skill of your men and
need to be trained."

"We will be proud to serve you," replied Robin.

"As for that despicable Sheriff of Nottingham," said King Richard, "he will receive no pardon. He will receive his due."

The Sheriff of Nottingham was publicly disgraced. The pompous man was stripped of his office and was placed in the stocks for all to mock.

King Richard returned to the throne and restored justice to the land. Robin, Marian, and their finest archers accompanied the king to London. For a time they trained soldiers in the use of the longbow. Before long, though, they tired of the city, for their hearts had remained in Sherwood Forest. They missed the sunlight glistening through the immense trees and the woodland animals scurrying about. Eventually, they returned to Sherwood to spend the rest of their days amidst the beauty of the forest.